There are 30 different and awesome vehicles for you to discover in this coloring book!

We hope you have lots of fun coloring and doodling :-)

_____

Name of the artist

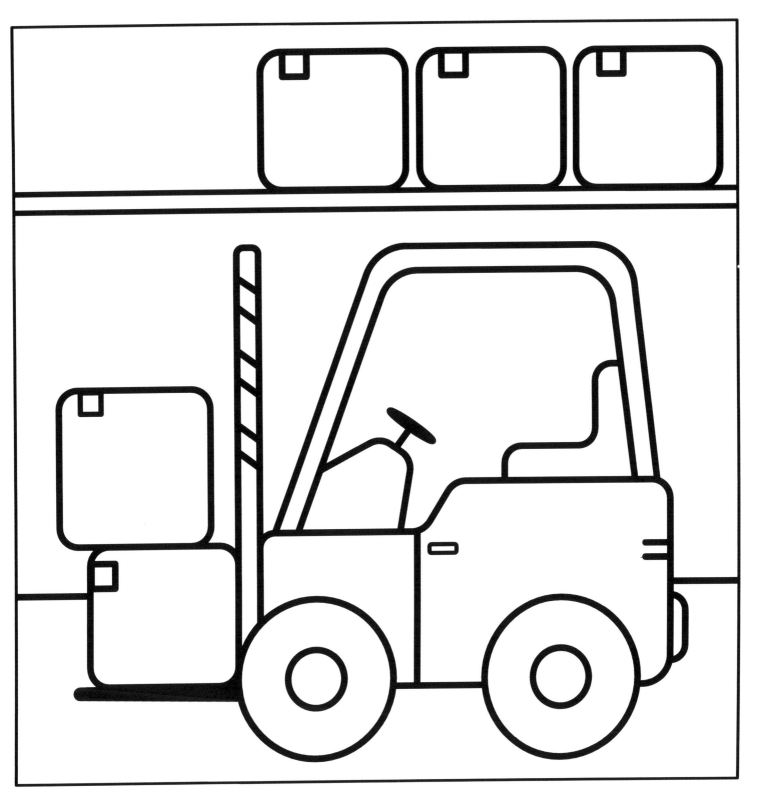

We hope you liked this book!

It would mean a lot to us to receive feedback, praise or criticism in form of a rating on Amazon or via e-mail at booksbykwabu@gmail.com.

THANK YOU!

:-)

ISBN: 979-8702936093

Imprint:

Kwabu LLC

Attn: Wes Holmstrom

PO Box 1023

Refugio, TX 78377

Made in the USA
Columbia, SC
19 December 2024

49998131R00037